Happy Birthday,
Blue Kangaroo!

Emma Chichester Clark

HarperCollins *Children's Books*

for Anna
and
Eliza

Have you read these picture books by Emma Chichester Clark?

I Love You, Blue Kangaroo!

Where Are You, Blue Kangaroo?

It Was You, Blue Kangaroo!

What Shall We Do, Blue Kangaroo?

I'll Show You, Blue Kangaroo!

Merry Christmas, Blue Kangaroo!

First published in hardback in Great Britain by Andersen Press Ltd in 2006
First published in paperback by HarperCollins Children's Books in 2008
This edition published in 2009

5 7 9 10 8 6 4

ISBN: 978-0-00-723231-4

HarperCollins Children's Books is a division of HarperCollins Publishers Ltd.

Text and illustrations copyright © Emma Chichester Clark 2006

Visit our website at: www.harpercollins.co.uk
Printed and bound in China

Blue Kangaroo belonged to Lily.
He was her very own kangaroo,
and they shared everything – even birthdays.
On their birthday, Lily woke up and said,
"Happy birthday to you, Blue Kangaroo!"

Lily and Blue Kangaroo were having a birthday party.
Lily had sent out pink invitations to all her friends.
"I want everything to be pink!" said Lily.

Lily put on her new pink dress, pink cardigan, pink socks and pink shoes. She put a pink ribbon on Blue Kangaroo.

Blue Kangaroo
wasn't sure if he liked it.

First, the triplets arrived, all in pink. They brought their pink furry bears and three pink presents.

Tallulah and Milly were next. They brought two pink presents and Milly's little brother, Tom, who wore pink rabbit ears.

Soon, everyone was there in their pink party clothes,
with their pink furry animals, and their pink presents.

Lily opened her presents.

"I am the only
one who is blue,"
thought Blue Kangaroo.

They played games. First, pass the parcel. Lily's little
brother collected all the pink wrapping paper.

Next was musical bumps, but Lily's little brother
kept taking away the cushions.

Then it was time for the magician.
He had a pink fairy helper.

He waved his magic wand and turned a pink handkerchief into a stream of pink ribbons.

Then he turned a white rabbit into a pink one.
All the children jumped up to see.

Lily went up and kissed the pink rabbit.

"I bet Lily wishes the magician could make me pink too," thought Blue Kangaroo.

When it was teatime, all the little girls (and three little boys) took their pink babies to have their birthday tea.

There were pink cakes and pink biscuits and pink
jellies. Then the curtains were drawn and the
lights turned out . . .

and Lily's mum came in carrying
the cake. It was a pink kangaroo!

Blue Kangaroo's
heart sank. "I've
got to do something!"
he thought.

When Lily saw the pink kangaroo, she was so excited
that she stood on her chair and shouted, "Hooray!
A pink kangaroo!"
Blue Kangaroo fell on the floor, but no one noticed.

Blue Kangaroo tiptoed out of the room, as everyone
sang happy birthday to Lily. He went towards
the kitchen.

He saw exactly what he was looking for.
It was just a skip and a hop away.
He jumped his best kangaroo jump . . .

. . . and landed in the bowl of pink icing!
But it wasn't the way he'd expected it to be, at all.

It was hard and it wouldn't stick.
Most of it fell off.
"It's hopeless," thought Blue Kangaroo.

He felt so miserable he thought he couldn't face
going back to the party, so he crept upstairs to
Lily's room.

At that moment, Lily said,
"Let's sing happy birthday to Blue Kangaroo!"
But he wasn't there.
"*Where* is he?" she cried.

Lily ran upstairs to look. She saw the pink footprints.
She saw the pink ribbon thrown on the floor.
She saw Blue Kangaroo lying on the bed, wrapped
in a blue sock.

Lily suddenly understood.

"Oh, Blue Kangaroo," she whispered. "You are such a beautiful blue. There is nothing nicer than blue. I wish I was blue, like you!"

She took off her pink dress and her pink cardigan.
She took off everything that was pink.
Then she dressed herself in blue.
"I love blue and I love you!" said Lily.

The party was nearly over, so Lily said thank you to
everyone for her presents.
"I just want to say that I really love pink, *and blue*,
and thank you very much!"

"Can I say goodbye to Blue Kangaroo?" asked Milly.
"Can I be next?" asked Tallulah.
"Please, please, can we?" asked the triplets.